Dear Parent:
Your child's love of reading starts here!

Every child learns to read in a different way and at his or her own speed. Some go back and forth between reading levels and read favorite books again and again. Others read through each level in order. You can help your young reader improve and become more confident by encouraging his or her own interests and abilities. From books your child reads with you to the first books he or she reads alone, there are I Can Read Books for every stage of reading:

SHARED READING
Basic language, word repetition, and whimsical illustrations, ideal for sharing with your emergent reader

BEGINNING READING
Short sentences, familiar words, and simple concepts for children eager to read on their own

READING WITH HELP
Engaging stories, longer sentences, and language play for developing readers

READING ALONE
Complex plots, challenging vocabulary, and high-interest topics for the independent reader

ADVANCED READING
Short paragraphs, chapters, and exciting themes for the perfect bridge to chapter books

I Can Read Books have introduced children to the joy of reading since 1957. Featuring award-winning authors and illustrators and a fabulous cast of beloved characters, I Can Read Books set the standard for beginning readers.

A lifetime of discovery begins with the magical words "I Can Read!"

Visit www.icanread.com for inform
on enriching your child's reading exp

To my wonderful little
Milo

I Can Read Book® is a trademark of HarperCollins Publishers.
Balzer + Bray is an imprint of HarperCollins Publishers.

Otter: I Love Books!
Copyright © 2019 by Sam Garton
All rights reserved. Manufactured in U.S.A.
No part of this book may be used or reproduced in any manner whatsoever without written permission except in the case of brief quotations embodied in critical articles and reviews. For information address HarperCollins Children's Books, a division of HarperCollins Publishers, 195 Broadway, New York, NY 10007.
www.icanread.com

Library of Congress Cataloging-in-Publication Data
Names: Garton, Sam, author, illustrator.
Title: Otter I love books! / by Sam Garton.
Other titles: I love books!
Description: First edition. | New York, NY : Balzer + Bray, an imprint of HarperCollinsPublishers, [2019] | Series: I can read! My first shared reading | Summary: Otter and his friends visit the library, where they discover that they can go anywhere and have as many adventures as they want by reading books.
Identifiers: LCCN 2018034252| ISBN 9780062845085 (hardback) | ISBN 9780062845092 (pbk.)
Subjects: | CYAC: Books and reading--Fiction. | Libraries--Fiction. | Otters--Fiction. | Animals--Fiction.
Classification: LCC PZ7.G211716 Omm 2019 | DDC [E]--dc23 LC record available at https://lccn.loc.gov/2018034252

19 20 21 LSCC 10 9 8 7 6 5 4 3
❖
First Edition

My First
SHARED
READING

I Can Read!

OTTER
I Love Books!

By SAM GARTON

BALZER + BRAY

An Imprint of HarperCollinsPublishers

We want to go on a fun trip!

I want to go to the circus.

Teddy wants to go to the sea.

And Giraffe wants to go

to a castle.

"Let's go to the library,"
says Otter Keeper.

"Is the library fun, like a
circus?" I ask.

"You will see," says
Otter Keeper.

The library is big.
There are lots
of books.

I get my own library card.

Otter Keeper says I can choose some books.

There are so many books!

I can't choose.

We ask for help.

I find a lot of books that I like.

"Sit down with me," says
Otter Keeper.
It is time to read.

The first book we read is
about the circus.

Reading about the circus
is fun!

The next book is about the sea.

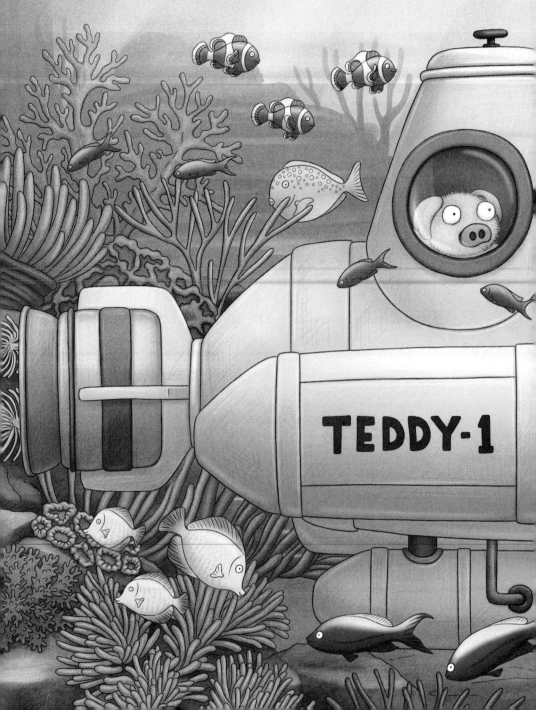

TEDDY-1

Teddy likes this book.

The next book is about a
magic castle.

Giraffe wants to read
this again.

23

The last book is about pirates.

We all pretend we are pirates!

Oh no, we have read all the books!

There are a lot more books
at the library.
We can choose more to
take home.

"Do you like the library?"

asks Otter Keeper.

"I love the library.
That was the best trip ever!"
I say.

We have had a busy day.

It is time for bed.

But we can't go to sleep yet.

We need to read
one more book!